A
"Thinking of Others"
BOOK

Wyatt's Wagon

⚙ ⚙ ⚙

BOOK TWO
Including Others

⚙ ⚙ ⚙

Written by GARY BOWER
Illustrated by JAN BOWER

TYNDALE HOUSE PUBLISHERS, INC. WHEATON, ILLINOIS

Acknowledgments

A project like this only deepens my love and appreciation for people in general. Specifically, I want to thank Jan, who makes writing (and living) more enjoyable every day; my son Nathan for his interest, time, and help in many ways; Anthony Weber for his insight and suggestions for improving this story; John Pianki for his encouragement and optimism; and the One with the biggest heart of all, who made a place for me.

— GARY BOWER

Many thanks to Justin Kraft for being such a cooperative "Wyatt"; to his mother, Dawn, for being so patient and flexible; and to Dad, who is as good a grandpa in real life as he is in a picture book. Thanks also to Jasmine Bower, Tynae Bower, Nikki Kaschel, Louis Kennedy, Clark Morgan, Levi Norris, Jennifer Pianki, and Shawn Price for sharing their refreshing personalities with all of us and for making me smile as I painted.

— JAN BOWER

Visit Tyndale's exciting Web site at www.tyndale.com

Wyatt's Wagon

Text copyright © 2001 by Gary D. Bower. All rights reserved.

Cover and interior illustrations copyright © 2001 by Jan Bower. All rights reserved.

Photo of Bower family copyright © 2000 by Christa McCrum. All rights reserved.

Photo of Gary and Jan Bower copyright © 2002 by G. Bower. All rights reserved.

Edited by Anthony Weber

Published in 2001 by Storybook Meadow Publishing, 7700 Timbers Trail, Traverse City, Michigan 49684.

Scripture taken from *THE MESSAGE.* Copyright © by Eugene Peterson, 1993, 1994, 1995. Used by permission of NavPress Publishing Group.

Library of Congress Control Number: 2001118176

ISBN 0-8423-7415-9

Printed in China

09 08 07 06 05 04 03 02

10 9 8 7 6 5 4 3 2 1

To our parents,
Bob & Edie Bower
and
Orley & Carol Norris,
who always found ways to make room

W yatt set his stuffed rabbit on the wagon. "Okay, Superbunny," he said, "here we go again." He pulled on the handle of the wagon, but as the wagon started to creep forward, the bunny tipped over and fell to the ground.

"Aw, c'mon, Superbunny," Wyatt complained. "I can't give you a ride if you won't sit still."

The bunny lay in the soft grass and stared at the clouds. He didn't really look like he wanted a ride. He looked like he wanted a nap.

Back into the wagon went the long-eared passenger, and away rolled Wyatt's wagon.

They followed a bumpy tractor path that led to Grandpa's apple orchard. The path took them up a long, gentle hill. Wyatt paused at the top, then trotted down the hill with his wagon rattling right behind him. *"Wheeee!"* he squealed.

He started back up the hill. "This time I'm riding too," he said, looking back at his bunny. But the bunny was gone.

"Where did you go, Superbunny?" Wyatt called. He looked all around. "Oh, there you are!" The stuffed animal was halfway up the hill, lying facedown in the grass.

Wyatt picked up his fuzzy friend and brushed him off. "Were you trying to fly or something?" he joked.

Shaking his head, Wyatt placed the clumsy creature in the wagon once again.

"Beep, beep! Look out!" someone shouted. Wyatt looked up to see a dark-haired boy running down the hill and pulling a strange wagon behind him. Wyatt moved his wagon out of the way just in time as the speeding wagon zoomed past. It rolled to a stop at the bottom of the hill.

The strange wagon had a big cardboard top. It reminded Wyatt of the covered wagons that pioneers used in the old days.

"I've *got* to do that again!" said an excited voice from inside the covered wagon. A grinning boy wearing a baseball cap poked his head out. "Take me back to the top, Aaron," he said.

"No way, Dustin," the other boy replied. "It's your turn to be the horse."

Wyatt knew them both. The wagon belonged to Dustin, the boy with the baseball cap.

Dustin climbed out and Aaron crawled in. "We're gonna be coming down again, Wyatt," Dustin warned, "so you'd better keep your little wagon out of the way."

Wyatt glanced down at his own wagon. It seemed very small.

"How about if we all ride down the hill together in yours?" he suggested.

"Sorry," Dustin answered, "but there's only room for one, and after Aaron it will be my turn again."

Wyatt sized up the wagon. It seemed huge to him, certainly big enough to hold at least two boys, if not all three of them. But there was nothing he could say. Dustin didn't want to make room, and it was his wagon.

Disappointed, Wyatt slowly shuffled down the path. Superbunny rode silently behind him.

Soon he could see Grandpa's red-spotted trees. The sweet smell of apples that drifted from the little orchard made Wyatt's mouth start to water. Standing on a ladder, Grandpa whistled a happy tune as he picked apples and put them in a bushel basket. Wyatt hurried to join him, stopping only when Superbunny took another tumble off the bouncing, rattling wagon.

"G'mornin'!" Grandpa called out. "Beautiful day for pickin' apples."

"May I help?" Wyatt asked.

"Of course," Grandpa said cheerfully.

Wyatt began picking from the lowest branches while Grandpa did the high ones. Before long the basket was full.

"These apples sure look good," said Wyatt.

"They taste even better," Grandpa replied with a wink.

That was all Wyatt needed to hear. *CRUNCH!*

Grandpa looked at the basket. "That's what I call a load," he said, "but I'm sure not excited about carrying that heavy basket clear back to the house."

"I brought my wagon," Wyatt offered.

"Why, so you did," said Grandpa. "Well, in that case, we can probably pick a few more." He lifted the basket onto the wagon, and they both went back to their picking.

"Move over, Superbunny," said Wyatt, dropping a handful of apples into the wagon. Soon the wagon was so full that some of the apples rolled off.

Grandpa stroked his chin. "I think we picked more than your wagon can hold," he said. "Looks to me like there's only one thing to do." He began to take off his jacket.

Wyatt looked puzzled. "Should we dump some out?"

"No need for that," Grandpa said. "We'll *make* room!"

And that's just
what they did.

At Grandpa's house, Wyatt was surprised to see his cousin, Tessa, sitting on the back porch. Their friend Luke was catching grasshoppers.

"I'm the princess," Tessa explained, "and Luke is my royal hunter."

Grandpa chuckled as he emptied the load of apples into a big wooden crate.

"Mother's in the kitchen helping Grandma make applesauce," Tessa told them.

"Well, then," said Grandpa, "we'd best go back for another load. Fetch a few more baskets from the barn, Wyatt, and I'll meet you in the orchard."

"May we come?" asked Tessa.

"Okay," Wyatt replied.

"Race you to the barn!" shouted Luke.

The children ran across the yard to Grandpa's barn. The big sliding door was open.

"Wow," said Luke,
"look at all this junk!"
"It's not junk," Wyatt
corrected him. "It's *stuff.*"
"Yeah," Tessa agreed,
"important stuff."
"But how does he fit
it all in?" Luke asked.
"He's really good at
making room," said Wyatt.
"Yeah," said Tessa.

They stacked three baskets
on Wyatt's wagon. Superbunny
rode in the top one. His ears flapped
and the baskets bounced as the children
made their way through the field.

"Grandpa said to pick from the low
branches or pick up good apples that
are on the ground," Wyatt told them.
"He doesn't want us to climb the ladder."

Standing on his wagon, Wyatt could reach plenty of apples. Luke and Tessa started gathering the ones that had dropped from the trees.

"Applesauce apples don't have to be perfect," Tessa said. "That's what Grandma says."

"What if they're rotten and have worms?" Luke wanted to know.

"I don't think they want *worms* in their applesauce," Wyatt said.

"Oh," said Luke. He threw the apple he was holding into the weeds.

"Do you think all three baskets will fit in the wagon?" Tessa asked.

Luke bit into a big, juicy apple. "Probably not," he slurped.

"I'm sure they will," Wyatt assured them. "Grandpa will make room somehow. He's really good at that."

Chrrr-guh, chrrr-guh, chrrr-guh, chrrr-guh! Something was rumbling through the tall weeds. They turned their heads back and forth, looking all around to see where the gruff, chugging noise was coming from. It grew louder and louder.

CHRRR-GUH, CHRRR-GUH, CHRRR-GUH, CHRRR-GUH!

Wyatt recognized that sound. "It's Grandpa's tractor!" he shouted. "And look! He's pulling a huge wagon!"

"Wow!" said Luke. "He *is* good at making room."

With Grandpa's help, they filled the baskets in no time and loaded them on the big wagon. The children climbed aboard too.

"No standing," said Grandpa. "We don't want anyone hurt."

Wyatt sat in the back of Grandpa's big wagon and held on to the handle of his little wagon. Away they went: the tractor first, the big wagon next, and Wyatt's wagon last.

"Let's go the long way!" Grandpa hollered over his shoulder. He drove along his property line by several neighboring houses. Wyatt waved at a boy who was swinging in his backyard.

"Hi, Cody!" Wyatt called loudly. Cody grinned and waved back.

"Grandpa, could Cody please ride with us?" Wyatt asked.

"We've got plenty of room," Grandpa said, stopping the tractor. "If he gets permission, it's fine with me."

Cody's mother said that he could, so Cody climbed aboard. "This is like a train," he said.

"A wagon train!" Tessa giggled.

Next they saw Jenna, Megan, and Dustin's sister, Ivy. They were jumping rope.

Grandpa stopped the tractor again. "Would you like a ride around the orchard?" he offered.

"Sure!" their voices sang out.

"Then go ask your parents," Grandpa said. "We'll wait for you."

Wyatt rushed to the front of the wagon. "But Grandpa," he said, "they're *girls.*"

"I'm a girl," Tessa reminded him.

"Nuh-uh," said Wyatt. "You're my cousin."

"I never met anyone that didn't enjoy a tractor ride," said Grandpa, "including girls. The more the merrier, don't you think?"

"I think so," said Cody.

"I shink sho too," said Luke with a mouthful of apple.

"I guess you're right," Wyatt agreed.

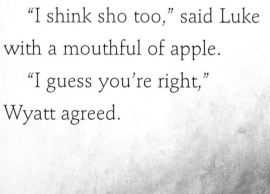

So Wyatt, Tessa, Luke, Cody, Ivy, Jenna, and Megan rode with Superbunny and the three bushels of apples in Grandpa's big wagon. Wyatt held the handle of his wagon tightly as it trailed behind like a caboose.

"Is that your wagon?" Ivy asked him.

"Yes," said Wyatt.

"It's nice," she said. Then she added, "My brother Dustin has one too."

Wyatt sighed. "I know."

Grandpa took them around the orchard, past the barn, and through the field. They stopped at the top of a hill.

At the bottom of the hill sat Dustin and Aaron. They didn't look happy at all. Dustin's beautiful covered wagon lay on its side. One of the wheels had come off.

Slowly, Grandpa drove the tractor down the hill and pulled up alongside the sad boys. "Are you two okay?" he asked.

"We're fine, thanks," said Aaron.

"But my wagon isn't," Dustin moaned.

"We can fix that back at the barn,"
Grandpa said. He turned to the kids
behind him. "Do you have
room for two more
back there?"
"I think so,"
said Wyatt.
"Is there room for my brother's
broken wagon?" Ivy asked.
"We can't leave it here."
"Where?" said Cody.
"It's getting sorta crowded."
"Yeah," Luke agreed.
"I'm already squished."
Wyatt spoke up. "Well, looks
to me like there's only one thing
to do. Isn't that right, Grandpa?"
Grandpa nodded.
"What?" everyone asked.

"We'll *make* room!" said Wyatt.

And that's just what they did.

Cody

Aaron

Ivy

Dustin

Luke

Jenna

Tessa

Wyatt

Megan

". . . and there's still room."
Luke 14:22

Can you remember?

Can you name all the boys in the story? Can you name all the girls?

How was Wyatt related to Tessa? How was Dustin related to Ivy?

How were Wyatt's wagon and Dustin's wagon different?

What kinds of things rode in Wyatt's wagon?

Who made room in his wagon? In his barn? In his heart? Who didn't make room?

What do you think?

Why do you think Dustin didn't let Wyatt ride with him?

What do you like about Wyatt's Grandpa?

Can you remember a time when someone didn't include you? How did you feel?

Do you know a big-hearted person who makes room for others?

Who do you know that could use a big-hearted friend like you?

In what ways can you include that person?

A Word from the Author to Parents and Teachers

I couldn't bear the image in my rearview mirror as my car crept down the driveway. Three sad little faces watched from the front porch, tugging at my heart like gravity. The next thing I knew, I found myself buckling in passengers.

Their beaming expressions and chattering voices were magical as we drove to the store. *Such excitement about picking up a gallon of milk and a loaf of bread,* I mused. Suddenly, I realized that the atmosphere in the car was much different from the one I would have experienced all alone. I noticed that, after a hard day, their cheerfulness was massaging my tired soul.

I had almost missed the experience altogether. And for what? Why did I almost exclude them? I'm sure I had my reasons. Perhaps I didn't want them to slow me down, or maybe I didn't want them to compete with the radio talk show that I planned on enjoying. Maybe I just didn't want to bother with seat belts and car seats. Whatever I would have gained by leaving them home, however, certainly didn't compare with the joy that coming along gave to them, nor the joy that my children splashed on me in return.

Of course, we simply cannot include everybody at all times. Sometimes we just need to be alone. Other times, space, money, and time require us to set limits. On the other hand, sometimes we need to venture out of our safety zones, stretch our hearts, and reach out to others. Often, when we sacrifice a convenience, someone else reaps a blessing. We are wise when we exchange what makes us comfortable for what makes us better.

A parable inspired *Wyatt's Wagon.* In the Bible (Luke 14:15-23), a wealthy man prepared a great banquet. It was so great, in fact, that he had room and food enough to accommodate far more than his original guest list. So this huge-hearted man opened his banquet hall to the entire community—the poor, the needy, and the friendless. Seeing his wealth bring happiness to others made him happy.

God has been like that to me. I've been through poor times. I've experienced a wide variety of needs. There have been times when I've felt friendless. Yet, despite my condition or situation, his invitation came to me. It comes to all of us.

Wyatt's Wagon was written not to make children feel like they *have* to include others but to show them the joy that results when they do. My hope is to inspire many "Wyatts" and "Grandpas" to change their corner of the world, one life at a time, as they make room for others.